Freedom Child of the Sea

Written by
Richardo Keens-Douglas

Illustrated by
Julia Gukova

Annick Press Ltd.
Toronto • New York

Second printing, August 1996

Annick Press Ltd.

Annick Press gratefully acknowledges the support of the Canada
Council and the Ontario Arts Council.

Canadian Cataloguing in Publication Data

Keens-Douglas, Richardo
  Freedom child of the sea

ISBN 1-55037-373-0 (bound) ISBN 1-55037-372-2 (pbk.)

I. Gukova, Julia. II. Title.

PS8571.E44545F7 1994   jC813'.54   C94-931720-9
PZ7.K44Fr 1994

The art in this book was rendered in mixed media.
The text was typeset in Garamond.

Distributed in Canada by:
Firefly Books Ltd.
3680 Victoria Park Avenue
Willowdale, ON
M2H 3K1

Published in the U.S.A. by Annick Press (U.S.) Ltd.
Distributed in the U.S.A. by:
Firefly Books (U.S.) Inc.
P.O. Box 1338
Ellicott Station
Buffalo, NY 14205

∞ Printed on acid-free paper.

Printed and bound in Canada by
Friesens, Altona, Manitoba.

Take pride
take time, take care, give love
be yourself
God never makes mistakes

Richardo Keens-Douglas

One day, not long ago, I went down to the beach to take a swim. It was a cloudy day and I knew it was going to rain. The beach seemed almost deserted. Only people like me, who love the rain, were there.

I was swimming and the rain started to come down. The drops were cold, so I dived under the warm sea water to shelter from them and

listen to them beat on the surface. It was a nice, quiet sound. Under the water I saw something swimming very fast in the distance. I started to panic, thinking, "Shark!" and I opened my mouth in fright and swallowed enough water to fill a jug. I choked and gasped and struggled for air.

Then all of a sudden I felt something wrap around my ankles and push me to the surface. When I got above the water and caught my breath I looked around for a fin. But to my surprise I saw a little boy, with the most beautiful angelic face you have ever seen. His skin was smooth as silk, and when he smiled his teeth were as white as sea shells. He swam in a circle around me and kicked his feet and burst out of the water, just like a dolphin.

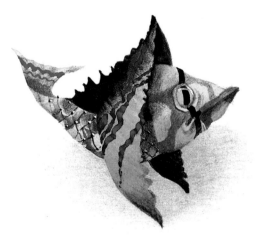

And when I saw him there I noticed that from the neck down he was covered with welts and scars. It looked so painful, yet he was smiling with his beautiful, smooth face.

Suddenly he just shot up into the air and dived into the water, and did not come up again. I swam back to the beach and lay on the sand and thought about what had just happened. The rain had stopped and the sky was sunny and blue.

An old man was walking down the beach towards me with a coconut
frond in his hand.

When he reached me he asked if I was all right, and I told him what had just happened. He smiled, laid the branch on the sand and sat next to me, saying,

"Ah, you are a lucky man, you were saved by the Freedom Child of the Sea. He bears all the pain and bondage of the human race."

For a moment we were both silent. Then I asked him, "How come he lives in the sea?"

Gazing straight ahead, the old man began, "One of my ancestors was brought to this island on a ship. My grandmother told me this story:

'Once upon a time, a very long time ago, there was a place in Africa that was beautiful, rich and powerful, with kings and queens, princes and princesses.

The people lived happily and with pride.

'Then one day, on the calm blue sea, came some strangers.

'A different kind of people, they came in big ships from a land far, far away. The people of the beautiful land believed that the strangers came with good intentions, so they opened their hearts to them. But the strangers came not to give, nor to share. They had come to take. And what they wanted were the humans.

'The strangers bribed some of the local people on the shore, with promises of goods and money, to go out and capture healthy young women and men and hold them for sale to the merchants who had come with the ships.

'And so mothers were separated from their sons, fathers from daughters, brothers from sisters. The wind that first day blew with a roar that had never been heard before in the beautiful land. It carried the sounds of fear, pain, tears and broken hearts out to sea.

'The captured people were told they were going to a new world. They were herded on and crammed into the bellies of these big ships, the men shackled, with chains on their ankles, wrists and necks. They had become slaves, and they were leaving their home.

'It was a very long journey to this new world, and the strangers crowded as many people onto these ships as they could. So there were people everywhere. They were beaten. They couldn't breathe in the stale air, with the decks hot and filthy, and it was very dark in the bellies of these ships. Many slaves died and were thrown off the side of the ships, without even a prayer said for them.

'Now, on one of these ships there was a woman. She was tucked away in a dark corner of the deck. Separated from her husband in Africa, she did not know which ship he was on or if she would ever see him again. This woman was going to have their first child. As the weeks went on she grew weaker and weaker, because the food was poor and the conditions unbearable. One day one of the young slaves overheard the sailors saying that she would not survive. When he heard that, he passed the news along to the others, and they plotted to hide her, but they could not move and there was nowhere she could go.

'Two days later the sailors came below. The slaves shouted that she was alive and that they would share their food and water with her, but their cries were in vain. The sailors took her up on deck and threw her over the side of the ship.

'Miraculously, as her body hit the water, the silky wetness caressed her skin. It was the softest touch she had felt since being taken from her home. And as her body slowly sank, with her last loving breath she gave birth to a baby boy, and together they gently floated to the bottom of the ocean.

'We call that boy Freedom Child of the Sea. They say he lives there with his mother and that his body is covered with welts and scars for all the pain his people suffered. He would carry these scars on his body as long as there is oppression and cruelty in the world. On the day his body is as beautiful as his face, from head to toe, you would know there is true freedom, compassion

and harmony among all the people. Then he will be able to walk out of the sea with his mother and live on the land like you and me. But until that day comes, they will live forever in the sea.' So when you are swimming and you feel the silky water lapping at your body, just remember it is Freedom Child, gently playing with you."

The old man had finished, and calmly looked out at the water.

"You said 'they will live forever in the sea'— is there no hope?" I asked.

"I believe there is hope for all of us." And with that he continued on his way. For my part I got up and ran home to tell this story to my family.

Other books by Richardo Keens-Douglas:

The Nutmeg Princess
La Diablesse and the Baby